Haunted Harvest

A collection of eerie poems
To celebrate Halloween.

Richard J. Anderson

First Edition
September 2013

Published by Richard J. Anderson

To my wife Cindy,
Who always indulged my love of Halloween.

III

IV

The Poems

Haunted Harvest

Introduction

The fall season has always been a special time of year for me. I carry wonderful memories of Halloween from my childhood in Ohio and of my mother relating the most amazing ghost stories to our family. Our house would be decorated for the season and she would begin her story-telling which truly brought out the magic for me and my siblings. I have to give her full credit for my love of this glorious time of year.

As the years went by I never lost my passion for the fall season and Halloween. If anything, my appreciation of it increased over the years. I would always find as much time as possible, starting in late September, to begin enjoying the fall season as it made its way towards Halloween. In the late 80's I started collecting some of the books that meant so much to me as a child. Helen Hokes' "Witches, Witches, Witches" and "Spooks, Spooks, Spooks" as well as Wilhelmina Harper's "Ghosts and Goblins". These books left an indelible impression on me and I would check them out from the local library every Halloween when I was a kid. It was a tradition that I never forgot! Even though they have been out of print for years, I think you can still find them on eBay now and again.

Years passed and I felt I the need to write my own Halloween book. I began writing Halloween poems in the late nineties and would share them with family members at our annual Halloween parties. It seemed I had a natural affinity for this form of poetry and would find that the work would flow easily, especially during the fall season. After several years I had enough to start assembling this book but I didn't want to publish it until I had illustrations to accompany the poems.

I felt I needed to do my own art and illustrations for this book. I loved those old Halloween books from my childhood that had great poems and stories with amazing illustrations. I would gaze at those old etchings and ink drawings over and over again as I read the poems and stories. The combination had an enchanting effect on me and added to all the Halloween magic in my life. I admired the simple black and white images because they were spookier and more powerful as Halloween illustrations. Maybe the publishers found it was much cheaper and a less risky venture to publish this way but whatever was the motivation for the mono color illustrations, I'm glad for their decision. And this was the direction I wanted to go with my little book.

But as often happens, years went by and finding time to work on completing this project was hard to come by, but it was always in the back of my mind. So finally in 2013 I made a commitment, I made the time, did the artwork and put the book together...

My aim with these poems was to create an old-fashioned, eerie feeling for the reader. Some do, and others have a more contemporary flair still in keeping with this magical time of year. This book isn't just for children, but for anyone who has a true love of Halloween and the wonderful changes this season brings. I wanted to write a book with poems similar to the ones that meant so much to me when I was a boy, a mix of poetry reminiscent of my childhood favorites along with those that would appeal to devotees of all ages.

I hope you're as happy with the result as I am.

Enjoy and Happy Halloween!

Richard Anderson 2013

Old Women

Tattered old women,
Shawl on her head,
I can see through her, but is she really dead?
Shuffling, shifting,
A sight that is not dear!
Wavy in the air, whisper in my ear.

Scream

Scream in a nearby room,
I pull the covers tight,
Am I afraid of a new and ghostly sight?
Are those footsteps coming near?
Must I again call an ancient gypsy seer?
Why can't I be alone in the middle of the night?
My heart is beating heavy and chest is damp and
tight.

Oak Trees

Oak trees in graveyards carry spirits though their
branches,
Yellow and brown leaves twist over families as they
grieve,
Roots that reach, coffins breach,
Flowers dry, ghosts that cry,
Branches sway on the cold dark day.

Halloween

Gentle breeze rustling the dry cornstalks,
A sound is heard a goblin walks,
A harvest moon suffers a black cat's cry,
Oh! Do the witches fly! Bonfire catches a pumpkins
gleam,
Rejoice it's Halloween!

The Thing

Black thing at my window, twisting a strange girth,
No form of life gave this fiend birth,
Pressing, eager in its way,
Hooks me with its eyes, from which it does not stray,
Frozen in my chair a certain numbness, I can't go!
As if my mind won't let me give up this horror show,
Its head, its mouth can sing?
Pressing, cracking,
Glass is such a fragile thing.

Divining

Divining ancient spirits in the middle of the night,
Julian Hotel, a small circle tight,
Henry my brother, and Jacob too,
Even our neighbor Jim had a hand in this,
All of us filled with supernatural bliss,
Now a spirit visiting, her name Virginia Hallen,
A lonely woman whose life was grey,
Trying to communicate of a bygone day,
Overwhelming sadness filling her still,
Buried rather deeply on a long forgotten hill,
Suddenly a sprit, dark opportunity to leave a final
mark,
Pressure overwhelming, contrast rather stark,
Creeping in my spine,
Candles shimmering and shake,
I feel a need to run,
Idle conjuring, no longer so much fun,
I throw the board into the fire and begin a
desperate run.

Soldiers

Pale costumed figures
At the side of the road,
Rifles, and shot guns and pitchforks,
A smell of old mold,
Angry intentions quickly my way,
Swift sounding footfalls, I hear their voices say;
Join us! Join us! You're just what we need.
They want me to join them, I feel it inside.
Awful feeling, new to me,
Surprisingly I hear myself say yes,
We'll see him; we'll see him bleed,
Under the forest's dark canopy of trees, we march and
march,
And taking no heed.
There is someone up ahead that needs to be taken, I
feel it.
The rain comes later, but I never awaken.

Stranger

The snow was falling heavy in that night,
I had to get home I didn't feel right,
The weather was powerful, indifferent to me,
I would get home, but how,
And then he,
The stranger was there,
He said I'll get you home; you can follow my footsteps
in the snow,
And off he went,
I hesitated, but was eager to go,
So I followed and he spoke no more,
I followed through the darkness not sure.
A moon overhead, and a sky of azure,
And then I noticed a light in the distance,
I was near and soon I was home.
I turned to thank him,
But in the cold air of my breath I was alone.

Eager

Candy corn and cupcakes on my plate.
Hurry mom, it's getting late!
All the candy might be gone before we start!
A growing excitement in my heart.
Growing excitement is not out of place!
I want to join the Halloween race!

A Warning

I told him to keep his eyes on the road,
To stay his lane and not press his luck,
Now our bodies are deep under muck,
And covered with mold.
Under the rock and broken clay,
With yellow roots and pockets of sand,
We're comfortable now and plan to stay.

Autumn Memories

Ohio's fall holds me still,
Memories of elbows high on a window sill,
Leaves of gold beginning and evenings cold,
Great anticipation of Halloween,
Excitement of costumes and witch's green faces,
Orange and black in so many places,
Carnivals with apples and piles of wet leaves,
Littering the yards,
A smiling postman with skeletons and pumpkins,
Delightful haunting cards,
Eating candied apples under a deep orange sun,
Blissful Halloween fun!
Not quite dark enough for trick or treat,
I'm pacing and hopping on excited feet,
Almost unbearable, with shouts outside,
I want to run in the street,
Feel the cold on my face, with a bag in my hand and
mist in my hair,
Love and secret knowing follows,
Before life's magic was covered with care.

The Rocking Chair

Our Victorian home has a room we won't enter.
Sounds of creeks and scratching and terribly more.
Strange echoes are heard nightly coming through
the floor
Of the room above our kitchen table,
A room where the rocking chair's stored.
We're all drawn to look, but know we're not able.
We keep eating and talking real loud,
We'll keep pretending there is nothing to hear.
We'll keep eating our dinners, and no, there is
nothing to fear.

The Garden

Our garden is special in the twilight,
If you're quiet and your eyes are keen,
If you keep a special patience and the time is just
right,
A visitor is seen,
A visitor with a message that no one knows,
He is not quite solid, a child's figure with his hands
outstretched,
There's a strange light about him, and his face often
glows,
He wants something as his mouth moves, but there
is never a sound,
He's not really frightening,
I almost embrace him, but there are no arms to be
found.

The Wind

There is more to the wind than most of us know,
The wind hides things from us as it pushes the air,
We have busy lives; we must get there fast,
We don't give it much care,
But there are things in the wind as it moves around us,
and moves things at night,
The are strange things in the wind not revealed by our
sight,
As the wind moves the trees and the leaves,
And whatever it can,
The wind has its own motives as it covers the land.

The Ghost

There's a thing in this old house that I must call a
ghost,
It comes nightly down the long hallway,
I dread it the most
I see it most often near the bottom of the stairs,
An undulating mass of a self contained cloud,
I'm more than terrified by it, I keep praying out loud,
I sit by the stone fireplace hoping it won't come again.
The crack of the wood, no relief to my mind,
I know it's there, or more of it's kind,
What does it want? I'm afraid I might know,
I won't think more about it,
Yes, I'm terrified, I won't be a liar!
But it's here in my house and I've got wood for the
fire.

Made in the USA
Las Vegas, NV
19 October 2023

79339115R00024